Dear mouse friends,
Welcome to the world of

MINI MYSTERY 2

THE RODENT'S GAZETTE
EDITORIAL STAFF

Geronimo Stilton
A learned and brainy mouse; editor of *The Rodent's Gazette*

Thea Stilton
Geronimo's sister and special correspondent at *The Rodent's Gazette*

Trap Stilton
An awful joker; Geronimo's cousin and owner of the store Cheap Junk for Less

Benjamin Stilton
A sweet and loving nine-year-old mouse; Geronimo's favorite nephew

Geronimo Stilton

THE LAKE MONSTER

Scholastic Inc.

ISBN 978-0-545-10370-1

Based on an original idea by Elisabetta Dami.
www.geronimostilton.com

Published by Scholastic Inc., 557 Broadway, New York, NY 10012.

Text by Geronimo Stilton
Original title *Il mostro di Lago Lago*
Cover by Giuseppe Ferrario
Illustrations by Claudio Cernuschi (pencils and ink) and
Valentina Grassini (color)
Graphics by Michela Battaglin

Special thanks to AnnMarie Anderson
Translated by Julia Heim
Interior design by Becky James

Fingerprint on cover and page i © NREY/Shutterstock

12 11 10 9 8 7 6 5 4 3 2 1 12 13 14 15 16 17/0

Printed in the U.S.A. 132
First printing, November 2012

TURN ON YOUR TV RIGHT AWAY!

It was a warm spring morning. I was feeding my dear little fishy, Hannibal, when — Oh, pardon me, I almost forgot to introduce myself! My name is Stilton, *Geronimo Stilton*. I run *The Rodent's Gazette*, the most famouse newspaper on Mouse Island.

Now, where was I? Oh, yes, I was feeding Hannibal when the phone rang. I was so startled I accidentally dumped too much food into his tank.

"Geronimo, it's Thea. Turn on your TV right away! I'll call you back in a minute!" It was my sister, Thea. **What could possibly be so urgent?**

I had just hung up the phone when it rang again. As soon as I answered, I heard a shout so loud it made me knock half the fish food onto the floor.

"Grandson, it's me! Turn on your

TV **IMMEDIATELY**! Go on now, move those paws! I'll call you back in a minute!" It was my grandfather William Shortpaws, founder of *The Rodent's Gazette*. **What could possibly be so urgent?**

I was heading toward my TV when the phone rang again. I was so surprised I JUMPED into the air, and a good bit of fish food fell into my open snout.

"Hi, G! Are you WATCHING TV?"

"Blugh . . . phug . . . ptui . . . ptui . . . ," I responded, spitting out the fish food.

"What?!" she said. "Turn on your

TV right away! I'll call you back in a minute."

It was **Petunia Pretty Paws**! She is the most fascinating mouse I know. She's a TV journalist who has dedicated her life to defending the environment. **But what could possibly be so urgent?**

I had just picked up the remote control when the doorbell rang.

I tripped on the carpet, and the rest of the fish food went flying . . . everywhere!

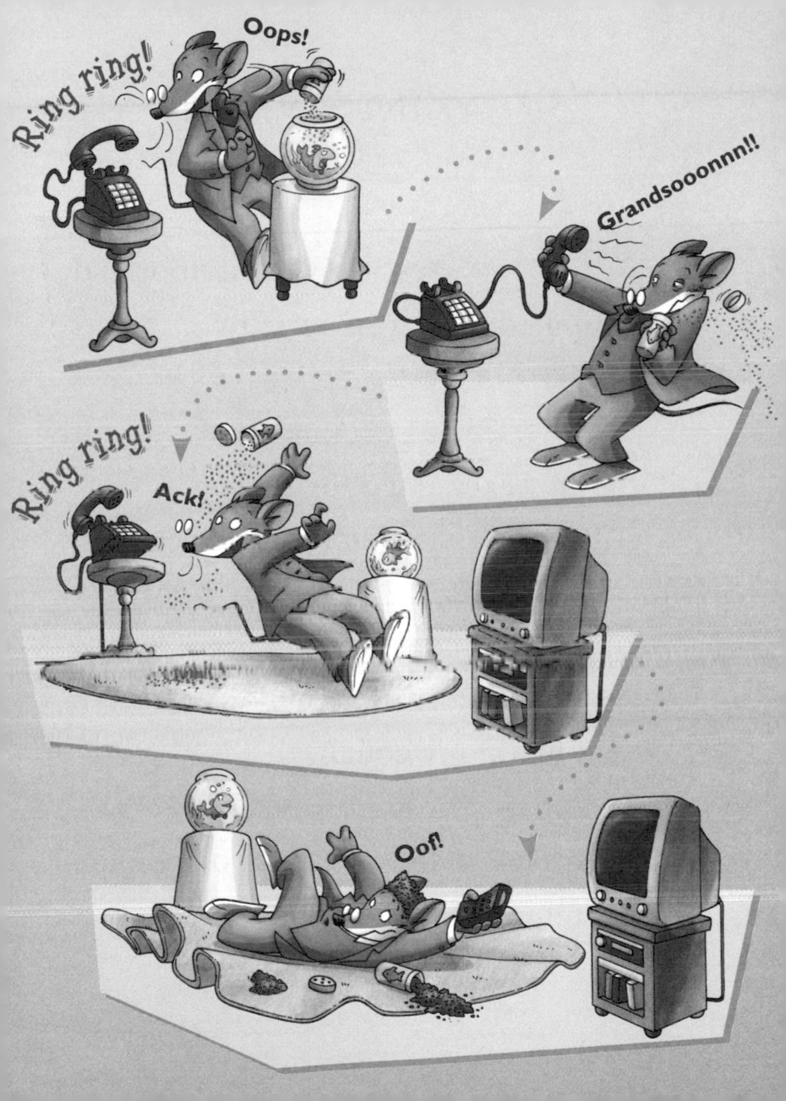
Oops!
Ring ring!
Grandsooonnn!!
Ring ring!
Ack!
Oof!

Breaking News!

I opened my front door and was immediately run over by two tiny CYCLONES!

"Hurry, Uncle Geronimo, turn on your TV!" they exclaimed.

It took me a moment to recover from my surprise. By then, my adorable nephew BENJAMIN and his friend Bugsy Wugsy, Petunia Pretty Paws's niece, were curled up on my couch.

"Hello, my little cheese niblets," I said affectionately. "Would one of you mind telling me wha —"

"Ssshh!" **hissed** Bugsy Wugsy.

I turned my attention to the TV screen. A newscaster was interviewing **Sally Ratmousen**, my number one enemy!

"When did you see the MONSTER for the first time?" the newscaster asked.

"As I said, a friend of mine who lives on the lake saw it yesterday, and he called

me **AT ONCE** to tell me about it!"

"Could you tell us what it looks like?" the newscaster asked.

"Listen, if you want to know that, I suggest you go buy the **special edition** of my newspaper, *The Daily Rat*. Right now! At once! Immediately!"

"Do you have **PHOTOS** of it?"

"Of course! There is a huge picture of the **LAKE MONSTER** on the front page!"

Oh, for the love of cheese! Had I heard correctly? A lake monster? And *The Daily Rat*, our rival newspaper, was coming out with a **special edition** about it? I had a feeling I'd be hearing from Grandfather William about this.

There's Not a Moment to Lose!

A split second later, the telephone began to **ring**. As I'd suspected, the first to call me back was Grandfather William. He was shouting even more loudly than before. "Hello, Grandson? Did you hear? You need to leave for the lake right away! Move it! **THERE'S NOT A MOMENT TO LOSE!**"

"But, Grandfather, you know I hate to travel. . . ."

It was too late to protest. He'd already hung up.

Next Thea called me back. "Gerry Berry, did you hear the news? We need to leave right away! **THERE'S NOT A MOMENT TO LOSE!** I'll be right over."

"But, Thea, you know I hate to travel. . . ."

It was too late to protest. She'd already hung up.

Petunia Pretty Paws was the last to call. "Hi, G! Did you hear? We can't miss out on a chance like this! It could be a rare animal we thought was extinct!

We need to leave right away. **THERE'S NOT A MOMENT TO LOSE!** I'll be right over."

This time, I didn't even try to protest. I hate to travel, but I would do anything for Petunia!

I was lost in a daydream about a **romantic** canoe ride with Petunia when I felt someone tugging at my **JACKET**. It was Benjamin and Bugsy.

"Uncle Geronimo, can we come, too?" asked Benjamin.

"I don't know, Benjamin," I said. "It could be **DANGEROUS**. . . ."

"Come on, Uncle G!" Bugsy pleaded. "Nothing bad will happen as long as you're there to protect us."

Their furry little faces were so hopeful I just couldn't let them down. So I **hugged** Benjamin and Bugsy and said, "Oh, all right. We'll go find the **LAKE MONSTER** together!"

Leaving for the Lake

We decided it would be best to **TRAVEL** together in Petunia's car. Since I am a true gentlemouse, I let Thea sit in the front seat, while I climbed in BACK with Bugsy, **BENJAMIN**, and all our baggage.

"Are you comfy, Geronimo?" asked Petunia, looking in her rearview mirror.

"**Mpffh . . .**

fllbb!" I responded. My snout was full of the synthetic cat fur on Thea's suitcase.

Petunia gave me a funny smile. "You know, G, you're squeaking very strangely today."

"That's because my brother is a very strange mouse," Thea declared. "Don't tell me you've never noticed."

Petunia and Thea took turns driving. They spent the whole ride chatting, while Benjamin and Bugsy passed the time playing Rat, Paper, Scissors.

Petunia stopped three times to let us stretch our paws. For me, that turned out to be three times too many!

At the **first stop**, I had to unload and reload all the luggage to get Petunia's notebook from the very bottom bag.

At the **second stop**, I had to change a flat tire all by myself while Petunia and Thea just stood there yammering away.

At the **third stop**, everything went smoothly . . . until we tried to leave, that is. We ran out of gas, and I had to push the car the rest of the way!

But for Petunia, I would have climbed CHEDDAR CRAG with one paw tied behind my tail. And without complaining, either!

At the Golden Catfish

At the lake, there was a nasty surprise waiting for us: Every TELEVISION STATION and newspaper on Mouse Island had sent REPORTERS and **photographers**! Plus, many curious rodents were visiting. There were mice everywhere, and everyone was talking about the LAKE MONSTER.

We made our way to the only hotel in the area, THE GOLDEN CATFISH, where the rooms were going like hot cheese buns. Fortunately, Thea had reserved five beds ahead of time.

Islet
Castle ruins

Lake
Golden Catfish Hotel
Swamp

The hotel's **manager**, followed by two rodents who were as thin as string cheese, came to meet us.

"Good evening, *heh heh heh*! My name is **SAMUEL SWEETWATER**, and I am the manager of the Golden Catfish.

Welcome! Did you have a nice trip?"

"Yes, it was fabumouse!" my friends responded. I couldn't squeak a word since I was still trying to catch my breath after pushing the car.

"Is this gentlemouse with you?" Sweetwater asked, pointing to me.

"Yes, of coursc . . . *pant* . . . ," I responded. "My name is . . . *pant* . . . Stilton, *Geronimo Stilton* . . . *pant* . . . *pant* . . ."

"Geronimo Stilton? The famouse writer? It is a real HONOR to havc you here with us!" he said, shaking my paw vigorously. "This place really needs a bit of **publicity**, *heh heh heh*! I was

very lucky to be down by the lake LAST WEEK when the monst —"

"Last week!" I exclaimed. "But on the news they said that the MONSTER was first seen yesterday."

Sweetwater stammered, "Um — yes, that is — I meant to say — last NIGHT."

"And you were the one to contact Ms. Ratmousen?" I asked, finally able to free myself from his PAWSHAKE.

"Yes," he replied. "Sally — I mean, Ms. RatMousen — is an old acquaintance of mine. When she heard the news, she wanted to buy the exclusive rights to the story. She pays very well, you know."

"My newspaper pays very well, too," I said.

"Of course, *heh heh heh*!" Sweetwater sneered. "But you see, Mr. Stilton, I've known Sally — I mean, Ms. Ratmousen — for so many years that I immediately thought of her."

He was still squeaking when my cell phone rang. Grandfather William thundered, "Grandson, are you at the lake yet? **MOVE THAT TAIL!**"

"Yes, Grandfather, I —"

"It's about time! I've sent up a photographer. He's there, waiting for you. **SO MOVE THOSE PAWS!**"

"But, Grandfather, I —"

"No thanks necessary, Grandson!

You can show your gratitude by getting busy out there! I want **PICTURES** of this monster by **TOMORROW** night! **SO MOVE IT!**"

"Grandfather, can you listen for a —?"

But he had already hung up. Rats!

"If you follow me, I'll show you to your rooms, *heh heh heh*!" **SAMUEL SWEETWATER** said. He turned to the two thin rodents. "**ZIP! ZAP!** Take these bags inside."

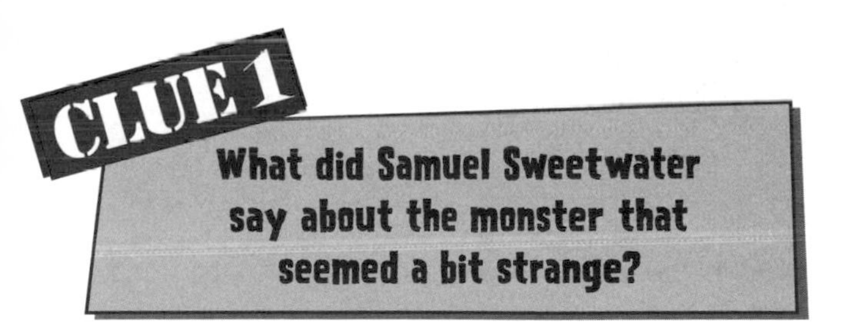

An Attic Fit for a King

As we headed to our rooms, Mr. Sweetwater turned to squeak with us. "Unfortunately, I only have one four-rodent room left. For the fifth, I thought of a **simple but comfortable** solution.

Like the gentlemouse I am, I accepted the "simple but comfortable" solution.

"Follow me to the **ATTIC**, Mr. Stilton."

"The *attic*?" I asked, lugging my bag up the **STAIRS**. Why, oh, why hadn't I stayed home?

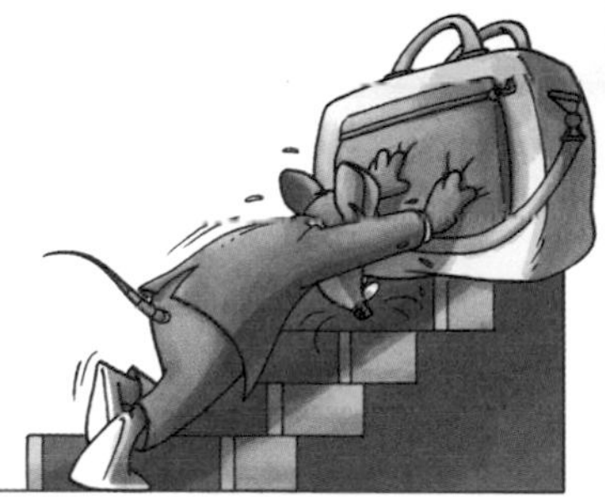

"The bathroom is on the first floor, only **ten flights of stairs** down. For an athletic rodent like yourself, I'm sure it will be nothing, *heh*! Naturally, the **HOT** water will cost you just a little bit extra. . . ."

Why, oh, why hadn't I stayed home?

"Is the bed **soft**?" I asked.

"The mattress is **natural straw**!

Just be careful of the holes in the roof — some BATS might come in. . . ."

Bats?!? Why, oh, why hadn't I stayed home?

Samuel Sweetwater threw open the door to the attic. "You and your roommate will do just fine here!"

As I stepped in, a powerful FLASH blinded me!

"My name is Stevie Snapson, and I never botch my shot!" my new roommate declared.

This had to be the photographer that Grandfather William had sent.

FLASH!
FLASH!
FLASH!
FLASH!

SALLY'S PHOTOGRAPHER

When I went down for dinner, more **unpleasant** surprises awaited me.

SALLY RATMOUSEN

was seated at the table next to ours. As soon as she saw me, she attacked. "Stilton! What in the name of cheddar are **YOU** doing here?"

"I'm here to photograph the **LAKE MONSTER**, Sally," I responded.

"You're a little **LATE**, old friend.

This time, I've got the scoop. LOOK!" She shoved a photo of the monster UNDER my snout. It was hard to see it too clearly because of the fog, but it really was quite striking.

"Let me introduce you to the author of this masterpiece," Sally declared. "This is Ricky Zoomson, my best photographer."

A scrawny rodent poked out from behind her. He shot me a smirk.

Trying to remain calm, I responded,

“Well, Sally, you’ve made the first move, but the next PHOTO will be ours. You can bet on it!”

“I don’t think so! Anyway, the MONSTER won’t show his snout until tomorrow at dawn,” Sally replied.

“How do you know that?” I demanded.

But she had already STOMPED away. This situation was getting stranger by the second!

I sat down at our table, but I couldn’t take my EYES off that photo of the monster. The more I looked at it, the more convinced I became that something wasn't right.

As soon as Petunia saw the photo, she **exclaimed**, "What an unusual-looking monster! There's definitely something **fishy** about it. . . ."

That worried me. "Do you think it could be **dangerous**?"

"Don't go all 'fraidy mouse on me!" exclaimed Thea. "We'll think about the **MONSTER** tomorrow. Let's get some shut-eye!"

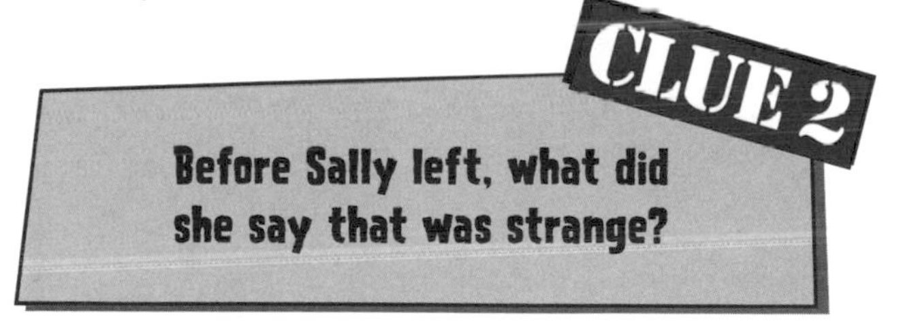

A BATHROOM, QUIIIIICK!

It wasn't a very peaceful night for me, dear reader. **Stevie Snapson** snored louder than my uncle Nibbles when he has a cold. Plus, anytime I managed to nod off for more than a few minutes, I dreamed of the **MONSTER**.

Suddenly, I had a *very urgent* need . . . to go to the bathroom!

I raced down ten flights of stairs, but tripped over the last step . . .

I raced down the **ten** flights of stairs that separated me from the first floor, but I tripped over the last **step** and landed in front of the hotel entrance.

Just when I thought there was no way I was going to make it, I saw a **yellow arrow** pointing to the bathroom.

I scurried in as quickly as I could!

That's when I heard some squeaking from the next room.

"Why do we need to wear oxygen

. . . and landed on my tail in front of the hotel entrance!

masks?" said a voice.

"Because this time the **MONSTER** will stay underwater. Only the head will appear. We can't let anyone see the **broken** tail!"

"Let's go. Boss said not to be late!"

I snuck out to see who was *talking*, but I must have just missed them!

Who were they? How did they know so much about the monster? And who was their **boss**?

The door was open, so I peeked inside the room. I spotted wet suits, flippers, masks, and other underwater **GEAR**. Things were getting **stranger and stranger**!

An Anonymouse Note

I raced up to the attic and tried to wake Stevie. No luck! Now his **SNORING** was louder than a marching band.

I sighed. I was tired, too. I tried putting my **pillow** over my head, but I could still hear him.

I turned this way and that, curling my tail around my ears to try to block out the sound. But I just couldn't sleep.

I was lying there with my **eyes** wide open when I noticed something.

Someone had SLIPPED an envelope UNDER the door. But who?

My whiskers were shivering with suspense. I quickly opened the *envelope* and scanned the note inside.

IF YOU BELIEVE IN THE MONSTER WHO LIVES IN THE LAKE, COME DOWN TO THE SHORE BEFORE DAWN BREAKS. IN FRONT OF THE CASTLE RUINS, YOU WILL GET TO SEE THE MONSTER – IN ALL OF HIS BEAUTY!

SIGNED,
A FRIEND OF YOURS

Something smelled **fishier** than day-old tuna. This **anonymouse** note told me so many details about the **MONSTER** appearing!

CLUE 3

Why does Geronimo think there's something suspicious about the note?

A Bumpy Ride

SUDDENLY, Stevie woke up. Instantly, he was clicking his FLASH button. "Where's the monster? Take me to him!"

I showed him the note. We decided we couldn't miss this chance to see the monster ourselves.

Outside, it was really foggy. We ran into MR. SWEETWATER in front of the hotel. "Can I give you a paw, Mr. Stilton?" he asked.

"We need to get to the other side of the lake, but our car is out of gas," I explained to him.

"Can you drive a motorcycle?"

"**I can!**" said Stevie.

The hotel manager smirked. "Don't worry, Mr. Stilton, it will only cost you a little bit extra, *heh heh heh. . . .*"

A few minutes later, I was buckled into the SIDECAR of an ancient motorcycle

as it zoomed over the bumpy dirt road that circled the lake. Stevie was in the driver's seat.

When we arrived at the other side of the lake, in front of the castle ruins, Stevie tried to BRAKE — but ended up crashing into an oak tree!

WHAT A CAT-ASTROPHE!!!

The motorcycle was totaled, but we were okay, thank goodmouse! And we'd made it. We were the ONLY ONES there! Now we just had to hope that the MYSTERIOUS note told the truth.

Suddenly, the lake water began to bubble. We could see something dark moving under the surface. . . .

THE MONSTER'S TAIL

A long, thick tail suddenly burst through the water's surface!

"Hurry, Stevie!" I yelled. "**Shoot! Shoot!**"

At that moment, a dozen other flashes went off. A herd of photographers popped out of the BRUSH. Everyone RACED for the lake as if they had a pack of hungry cats on their tails. **Sally's** photographer Ricky Zoomson pushed me so hard I ended up in the water! The monster's twitching tail missed me by a WHISKER.

I thrashed and splashed my way back to shore. By then, the **MONSTER** had disappeared under the waves once more.

The author of the **mysterious** note had tricked me. He had given everyone the same information. **THERE WENT MY EXCLUSIVE!**

A Strange Photo

We returned to the hotel on paw. Mr. Sweetwater greeted us with his usual smarmy **smile**. "Mr. Stilton, how'd you do on the motorcycle? *Heh heh heh!*"

I turned **pinker** than a naked mole rat. "Well, you see . . . that is . . . we got into a bit of a **WRECK**. . . ."

"Oh, don't worry about it," Mr. Sweetwater jeered. "We'll get it fixed in the blink of a cat's eye. It'll just cost you ***a little bit*** extra, *heh heh heh*!"

We went up to our room. While Stevie developed the **ROLLS** of film, I collapsed on my straw mattress and tried to get some sleep.

An hour later, we headed downstairs for breakfast. Thea was there with Benjamin and Bugsy, who **hugged** me. **Petunia** bounced over to me as well. "This place is a marvemouse **natural oasis**! We absolutely must prevent

anyone from **ruining** it. Especially now that the news about the **LAKE MONSTER** is everywhere."

"Did you get a photo of the **MONSTER**?" Benjamin asked.

I showed them the

photos. "Yes! Well, sort of . . ."

"You can see the monster in this one!" exclaimed **Bugsy Wugsy**. Or at least part of him . . ."

Stevie and I took a **closer** look. "See — I never botch my shot!" he exclaimed triumphantly.

I **gazed** and **gazed** at the photo: Something about the monster's ***tail*** seemed odd. But what?

CLUE 4

What looks odd about the monster's tail?

THE RAT RACE

The next day, every newspaper on Mouse Island had a **HUGE** headline about the Lake Monster on its front page. And they all **PRINTED** better photos than ours!

When my cell phone rang, I knew right away who it would be: **Grandfather William**.

"What is this rubbish we published, Grandson?!" he screeched. "You better not be cramping **Stevie's** style!"

"No, Grandfather, it's just that —"

"**NO EXCUSES!** Tomorrow I want a photo that's good enough to fill the entire front page. Do you hear me? **MOVE IT! GET THE PICTURE! GO!**"

When I ran into Sally Ratmousen, she waved the second **special edition** of *The Daily Rat* under my snout. "Watch and learn, Stilton, watch and learn! At *The Daily Rat,* we don't settle for a measly picture of a monster's tail! It's all or nothing, I say! This is a rat race, after all!"

When I looked at Sally's newspaper, I felt my heart sink all the way to my PAWS.

Suddenly, BENJAMIN exclaimed, "But this photo couldn't have been taken by Ricky Zoomson! Look where the castle ruins are. . . ."

We looked more closely at Sally's newspaper. BENJAMIN was right!

This whole story was starting to stink worse than rotten Gouda. It was time to uncover the truth!

CLUE 5

Why couldn't Ricky Zoomson have taken this photo with the other photographers?

THE DAILY RAT

THE LAKE MONSTER!

The Second Anonymouse Note

That night was even worse than the one before. Stevie was **SNORING** loud enough to wake a comatose cat. I just couldn't sleep!

All at once, I had a brilliant idea: I could figure out whom I'd heard in the room near the bathroom.

I went **DOWN** to the first floor. As soon as I entered the bathroom, I heard squeaking from the room next door.

"What do you mean, we need to go back **underwater**?"

"Well, the tail wasn't supposed to be

visible yesterday! It was all because of that CLUMSY rodent who fell into the lake. This time, the MONSTER'S HEAD WILL RISE out of the water. . . ."

They were the same voices as before! And they were squeaking about me!

I peeked through the keyhole and saw two rodents dressed in scuba gear.

Strange, very strange! I was sure I had seen those two before, but

couldn't remember where.

I crept out of the bathroom to follow them, but they had already disappeared.

Discouraged, I climbed back to the **ATTIC**. That was when I saw another ***envelope*** by the door.

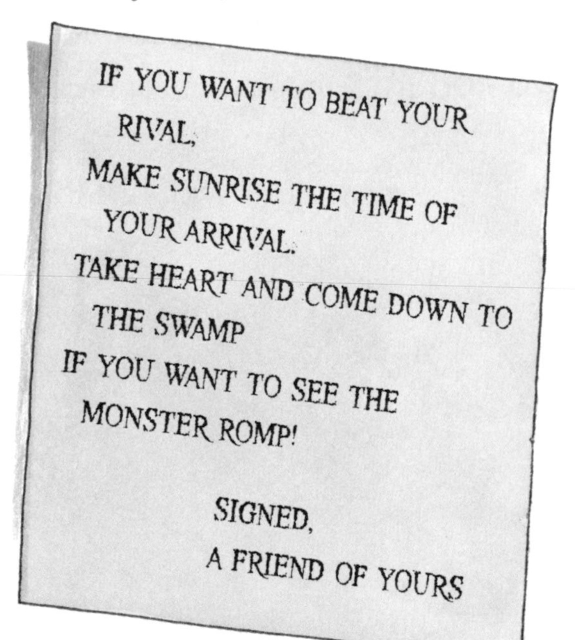

IF YOU WANT TO BEAT YOUR RIVAL,
MAKE SUNRISE THE TIME OF YOUR ARRIVAL.
TAKE HEART AND COME DOWN TO THE SWAMP
IF YOU WANT TO SEE THE MONSTER ROMP!

SIGNED,
A FRIEND OF YOURS

Mouseyback Ride on the Monster

Just before sunup, Stevie and I again stood at the entrance to the GOLDEN CATFISH.

SAMUEL SWEETWATER was also there, and asked me his usual question: "Can I give you a paw with anything, Mr. Stilton? *Heh heh heh!*"

"Can you tell me how to reach the SWAMP?" I asked timidly.

Mr. Sweetwater smirked as he replied, "Oh, it's easy. Just follow that path for about a mile. A TANDEM bicycle might get you there quicker. It'll cost you . . ."

"I know, I know," I said, rolling my eyes. "Just a little bit extra!"

After Stevie and I had pedaled for

about five minutes, the bike began to sink into the mud. We had to continue through the muck by paw. Blech!

The fog was so thick we could hardly see our paws. Then suddenly, the monster's back emerged from the water!

"Quick, Stevie! Shoot!" I shouted.

"Where? Where? WHERE?" he cried, taking pictures at random.

"Over there, on the lake!"

Once again, other photographers poked their snouts out of the shrubs and headed straight for the MONSTER. And Ricky Zoomson pushed me into the water AGAIN!

I was flailing around, when suddenly

the monster came up from the depths — and I found myself **on its back**!

"Stevie, **TAKE THE PICTUUUURE**!" I screeched. I was scared out of my fur.

The last thing I saw was the flash from his camera — at that moment, the monster flung me toward shore!

WHAT HAPPENED?

When I woke up, I was back at the hotel.

"How are you feeling, Uncle Geronimo?" Benjamin asked.

"All right," I mumbled, opening my eyes. "What happened?"

"You RODE the Lake Monster," Benjamin said. "Look!" He showed me the front page of *The Rodent's Gazette* with MY picture front and center.

"You see?" Stevie said proudly. "I told you I never botch my shot!"

"You were very COURAGEOUS, G!" said Petunia, making me blush. She is such a fascinating mouse!

My cell phone rang. As soon as I answered it, I heard Grandfather William's voice squawking: "Grandson, what a photo! Have you seen it? Snapson is worth his weight in cheese! I want more photos just like that, but clearer! Do you hear me? MOVE IT! SNAP THOSE PICS!"

Take a Look-See!

Well, Grandfather was happy, so at last I could relax! Thank goodmouse.

My relief didn't last long, since Sally Ratmousen soon burst into the room. "Stilton! Congratulations! You took a really nice photo!"

"Thank you, Sally," I responded with satisfaction. "As you can see, my newspaper is just as good as yours!"

"Oh, of course," she replied. "But my photographer is even better than yours. Didn't I tell you that I am always right? Take a look-see!" She shoved a

close-up photo of the MONSTER'S FACE under my snout. "That monster is mine, and I won't let you have him!"

With that, she left,

SLAMMING

the door behind her.

ANOTHER SLEEPLESS NIGHT

Stevie snored again that night. He was loud enough to wake a dead rat. As usual, I wasn't able to sleep a **wink**!

My mind was racing like a hamster on a wheel. I thought about the story of the monster, our attempts to photograph him, **SALLY'S** scoop, Mr. Sweetwater's strange behavior, and those two suspicious rodents in the room next to the bathroom. I was so confused. . . .

But I knew I needed to find those two rodents! I got out of bed, crept down the stairs, and headed into the bathroom.

It was then that my LUCK changed. From the room next door I could hear squeaks that I knew quite well by now.

"But, Sally, that's too dangerous!"

"I don't care!" Sally replied. "Are you telling me that simpleton Stilton can climb on the monster and I can't?! I want to be in a picture sitting astride the monster! RIGHT NOW! AT ONCE!"

"Okay, Sally, we'll meet at the center of the lake at MIDNIGHT on the dot," said Mr. Sweetwater. "You two, go get ready."

"You better not be late, not even by a minute — or else! Now get out, you cheeseheads!"

Then I saw Sally and Samuel Sweetwater leave the room, followed by the two scuba divers. At last, I'd figured out who they were!

I ran to wake up Thea, Petunia, Benjamin, Bugsy Wugsy, and Stevie. It was our turn to JOIN THE ACTION!

A Surprise from the Sky

An hour later, Stevie and I were in a life raft, smack-dab in the middle of the lake, waiting for the MONSTER to appear. It was a moonless night.

My tail was trembling with fright!

After a few minutes of silence, we heard the thrum of a motorboat

approaching at top speed. Its lights were off, so the rodents on board couldn't see us. But we could hear their voices.

"Hurry up! I don't want to catch a cold out here on your chilly lake!"

"Stay calm, Sally — Zip and Zap will be here any moment. *Heh heh heh!*"

"They better be!" Sally snapped. "Now, Ricky, try to get the shot this time. I'm tired of having to retouch your **abominable** photos!"

Suddenly, we heard a rumbling in the distance. The monster was approaching from the bottom of the lake!

"Get ready to shoot, Stevie, but only when I say so!" I whispered.

"Snapson never botches his shot!" he declared, standing up with his camera.

At that moment, a wave from the monster made the raft rock, and Stevie went snoutdown into the water! He hit the FLASH button on his way in, and the surface of the lake lit up.

Naturally, Sally noticed us. "*Stilton*!" she yelled. "Don't you know when to throw in the cheesecloth?"

I didn't answer — I was too busy trying to fish Stevie out of the lake!

Meanwhile, the MONSTER was getting closer. Just when it seemed like we were about to end up as his food, a HELICOPTER appeared above us. It was Thea and Petunia!

At last, I managed to pull Stevie back onto the raft, but by now the monster was practically on top of us!

That was when a ROPE ladder fell out of the helicopter and into my paws. Stevie and I grabbed it. We escaped the monster by a WHISKER!

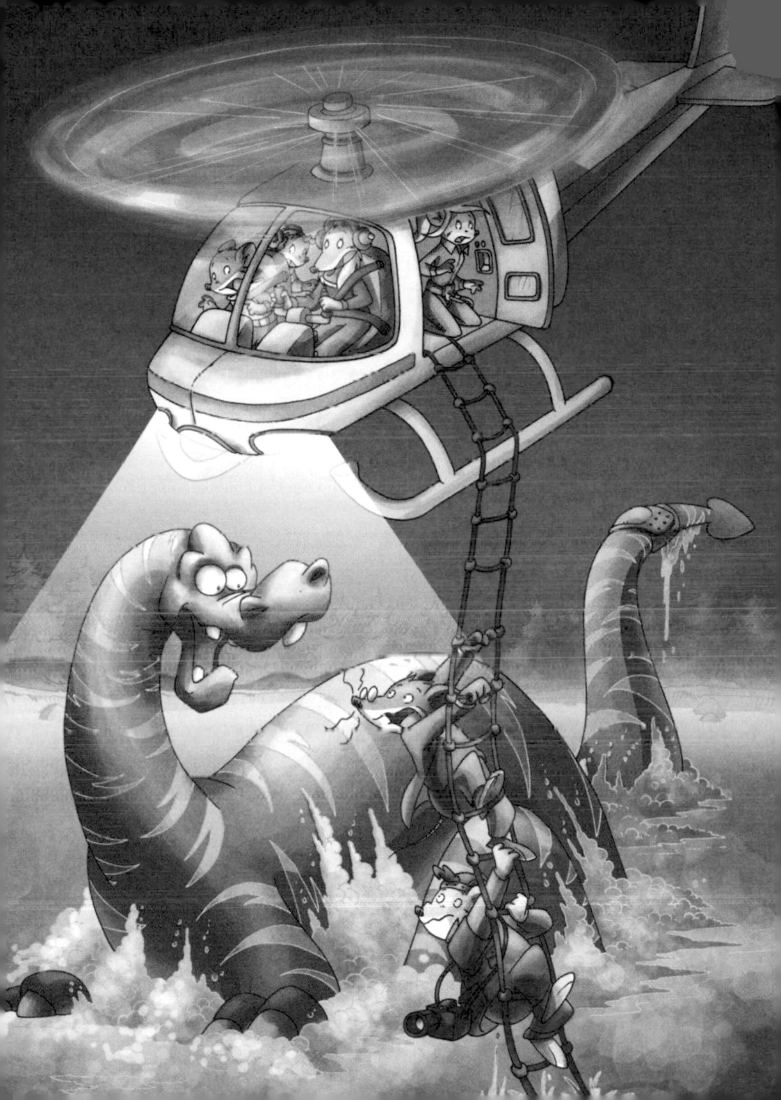

THE BELLY OF THE BEAST

Incredibly, Stevie had managed to photograph the **MONSTER** underwater!

"**See? Snapson never botches his shot! Never!**" he boasted.

The next day, the photo was on the front page of *The Rodent's Gazette*. In the article that accompanied it, I explained what that **SCOUNDREL** Samuel Sweetwater had done.

The monster was a **FAKE**! Samuel Sweetwater had cooked up this monstrous **SCAM** to get more tourists to come to the lake. He hoped to expand his hotel and

THE RODENT'S GAZETTE
Editor & Publisher: Geronimo Stilton
www.geronimostilton.com
17 Swiss Cheese Center
New Mouse City
MECHANICAL MONSTER
The secret of the Lake Monster
is revealed underwater!

make a small fortune.

And SALLY? Well, with the exclusive to the story, her newspaper would have SOLD millions of copies. But instead, it was *The Rodent's Gazette* that set a new sales record!

Samuel and Sally had to go to court to face fraud charges. A judge made them pay a huge fine. Thanks to a suggestion from Petunia, the money was used to help build a magnificent natural park at the lake. It became a wildlife preserve where rodents can play, hike, and go bike riding, WITHOUT DANGER!

Can you guess what the park's main attraction is? Riding around

the lake on the monster's back!
And guess who does all the pedaling to power the monster: Samuel Sweetwater, Zip, and Zap!

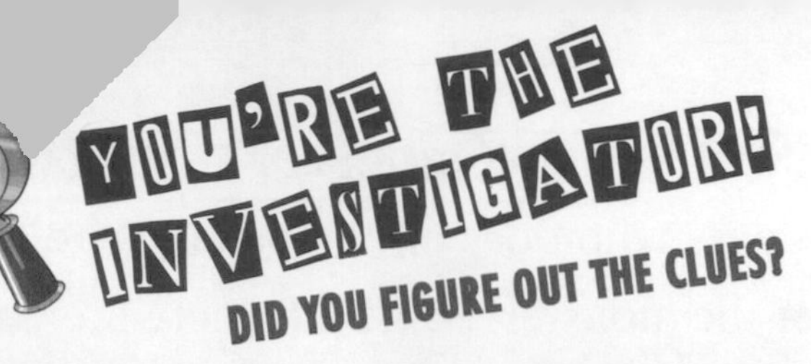

1 What did Samuel Sweetwater say about the monster that seemed a bit strange?

He said that he had seen it "last week," but Sally reported that the monster had first been seen just the day before.

2 Before Sally left, what did she say that was strange?

She said the monster would appear at dawn. How could she possibly know that?

3 Why does Geronimo think there's something suspicious about the note?

Because the author of the note knew where and when the monster would appear. How could he or she know that?

4 What looks odd about the monster's tail?

There's a bandage on the monster's tail! It's broken, just like the two rodents in the room next to the bathroom said.

5 Why couldn't Ricky Zoomson have taken this photo with the other photographers?

In the background you can see the castle ruins, but Ricky Zoomson was on the shore in front of the ruins. Therefore, this photo was taken at a different time and from a different spot on the lakeshore.

6 Do you recognize the two scuba divers?

They are Zip and Zap!

HOW MANY QUESTIONS DID YOU ANSWER CORRECTLY?

ALL 5 CORRECT: You are a SUPER-SQUEAKY INVESTIGATOR!

FROM 2 TO 4 CORRECT: You are a SUPER INVESTIGATOR! You'll get that added squeak soon!

LESS THAN 2 CORRECT: You are a GOOD INVESTIGATOR! Keep practicing to get super-squeaky!

Farewell until the next mystery!

Geronimo Stilton

Check out all my mini-mysteries!
Geronimo Stilton
THE SUPER SCAM
MINI MYSTERY
1
Geronimo Stilton
THE LAKE MONSTER
SCHOLASTIC
MINI MYSTERY
2
Geronimo Stilton
THE MOUSE HOAX
SCHOLASTIC
MINI MYSTERY
3

Don't miss any of my other fabumouse adventures!

#1 Lost Treasure of the Emerald Eye

#2 The Curse of the Cheese Pyramid

#3 Cat and Mouse in a Haunted House

#4 I'm Too Fond of My Fur!

#5 Four Mice Deep in the Jungle

#6 Paws Off, Cheddarface!

#7 Red Pizzas for a Blue Count

#8 Attack of the Bandit Cats

#9 A Fabumouse Vacation for Geronimo

#10 All Because of a Cup of Coffee

#11 It's Halloween, You 'Fraidy Mouse!

#12 Merry Christmas, Geronimo!

#13 The Phantom of the Subway

#14 The Temple of the Ruby of Fire

#15 The Mona Mousa Code

#16 A Cheese-Colored Camper

#17 Watch Your Whiskers, Stilton!

#18 Shipwreck on the Pirate Islands

#19 My Name Is Stilton, Geronimo Stilton

#20 Surf's Up, Geronimo!

#21 The Wild, Wild West

#22 The Secret of Cacklefur Castle

A Christmas Tale

#23 Valentine's Day Disaster

#24 Field Trip to Niagara Falls

#25 The Search for Sunken Treasure

#26 The Mummy with No Name

#27 The Christmas Toy Factory

#28 Wedding Crasher

#29 Down and Out Down Under

#30 The Mouse Island Marathon

#31 The Mysterious Cheese Thief

Christmas Catastrophe

#32 Valley of the Giant Skeletons

#33 Geronimo and the Gold Medal Mystery

#34 Geronimo Stilton, Secret Agent

#35 A Very Merry Christmas

#36 Geronimo's Valentine

#37 The Race Across America
#38 A Fabumouse School Adventure
#39 Singing Sensation
#40 The Karate Mouse
#41 Mighty Mount Kilimanjaro
#42 The Peculiar Pumpkin Thief
#43 I'm Not a Supermouse!
#44 The Giant Diamond Robbery
#45 Save the White Whale!
#46 The Haunted Castle
#47 Run for the Hills, Geronimo!
#48 The Mystery in Venice
#49 The Way of the Samurai
#50 This Hotel Is Haunted!
#51 The Enormouse Pearl Heist
Don't miss these very special editions!
THE KINGDOM OF FANTASY
THE QUEST FOR PARADISE: THE RETURN TO THE KINGDOM OF FANTASY
THE AMAZING VOYAGE: THE THIRD ADVENTURE IN THE KINGDOM OF FANTASY
THE DRAGON PROPHECY: THE FOURTH ADVENTURE IN THE KINGDOM OF FANTASY

About the Author

Born in New Mouse City, Mouse Island, **Geronimo Stilton** is Rattus Emeritus of Mousomorphic Literature and of Neo-Ratonic Comparative Philosophy. For the past twenty years, he has been running *The Rodent's Gazette*, New Mouse City's most widely read daily newspaper.

Stilton was awarded the Ratitzer Prize for his scoops on *The Curse of the Cheese Pyramid* and *The Search for Sunken Treasure*. He has also received the Andersen 2000 Prize for Personality of the Year. One of his bestsellers won the 2002 eBook Award for world's best ratlings' electronic book. His works have been published all over the globe.

In his spare time, Mr. Stilton collects antique cheese rinds and plays golf. But what he most enjoys is telling stories to his nephew Benjamin.

1. Main entrance
2. Printing presses (where the books and newspaper are printed)
3. Accounts department
4. Editorial room (where the editors, illustrators, and designers work)
5. Geronimo Stilton's office
6. Helicopter landing pad

THE RODENT'S GAZETTE

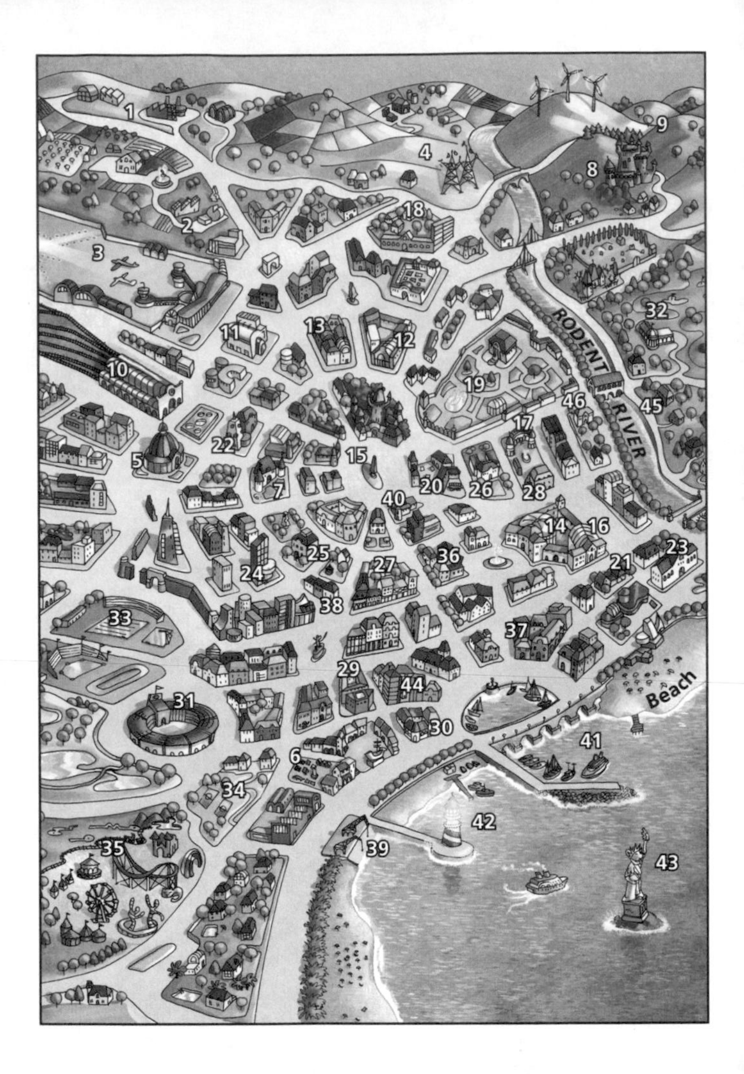
1
9
4
8
18
2
3
32
RODENT
13
11
12
10
19
46
45
RIVER
17
22
15
5
7
20
26
28
40
14
16
23
25
36
24
27
21
38
33
37
29
44
Beach
31
30
41
6
34
42
35
39
43

Map of New Mouse City

1. Industrial Zone
2. Cheese Factories
3. Angorat International Airport
4. WRAT Radio and Television Station
5. Cheese Market
6. Fish Market
7. Town Hall
8. Snotnose Castle
9. The Seven Hills of Mouse Island
10. Mouse Central Station
11. Trade Center
12. Movie Theater
13. Gym
14. Catnegie Hall
15. Singing Stone Plaza
16. The Gouda Theater
17. Grand Hotel
18. Mouse General Hospital
19. Botanical Gardens
20. Cheap Junk for Less (Trap's store)
21. Parking Lot
22. Mouseum of Modern Art
23. University and Library
24. *The Daily Rat*
25. *The Rodent's Gazette*
26. Trap's House
27. Fashion District
28. The Mouse House Restaurant
29. Environmental Protection Center
30. Harbor Office
31. Mousidon Square Garden
32. Golf Course
33. Swimming Pool
34. Blushing Meadow Tennis Courts
35. Curlyfur Island Amusement Park
36. Geronimo's House
37. Historic District
38. Public Library
39. Shipyard
40. Thea's House
41. New Mouse Harbor
42. Luna Lighthouse
43. The Statue of Liberty
44. Hercule Poirat's Office
45. Petunia Pretty Paws's House
46. Grandfather William's House

This way to the Rodent Straits
Brigand's Isle
Tomcat Island
Pirate Ship of Cats
Hamster Islands
Blue Dolphin Bay
Coral Reefs
This way to the Mousific Ocean
Stray Cat Harbor
Cat's Claw Bay
Panther Archipelago
Swissville
Cheddarton
Mouseport
San Mouscisco
This way to the Ratlantic Ocean
New Mouse City
Mousefort Beach
Furflung Island
This way to the Sea of Mice
MOUSE ISLAND
N
W
E
S
1
2
3
4
5
6
7
8
9
10
11
12
13
14
15
16
17
18
19
20
21
22
23
24
25
26
27
28
29
30
31
32
33
34
35
36
37